Speeding Down the Spiral

Speeding Down the Spiral

An Artful Adventure

By Deborah Goodman Davis

Illustrated by Sophy Naess

Library of Congress Control Number: 2012907537
ISBN: 978-0-9855568-0-8

Manufactured by Color House Graphics, Inc., Grand Rapids, MI, USA
October 2012
Job# 38556

This book is lovingly dedicated to my family, especially my mother, who inspired my enjoyment of art and museums. I would like to thank Lizzie, Ben, Zachary S., Julia, Andrew, Noah, Nathaniel, Lilah, Orly, Autumn, Gerry, Marla, Beth L., and Zachary L. for being my readers, and Charlotte, Clara, and Desirée for acting as models for the illustrations. Many thanks to Sophy, Joan, Erika, Jennifer, and Beth S. for their invaluable help.

On a sunny summer Sunday, Dad decided to take Lizzie and her baby brother, Ben, to an art museum.

"Being inside will give us some relief from the heat," he said, "and we'll see some cool art!"

"Sounds boring," said Lizzie. "I wish we were going to a water park!"

"This museum is awesome," said Dad. "It's shaped like a spiral!"

Why is a spiral awesome? wondered Lizzie. *Spirals make me dizzy! And how can I have fun if we have to push Ben's stroller everywhere?*

Lizzie looked up at the spiral as she entered the museum. The ramp reminded her of a giant curly noodle, and it made her feel hungry.

I wish I had something to eat, Lizzie said to herself. She searched in her pocket, hoping to find a piece of candy.

Lizzie, Ben, and their dad squeezed into the elevator. It took them to the very top floor.

When Lizzie looked down into the huge spiral, she felt like she was spinning! Then she noticed a tiny pool, shaped like an eye, at the bottom.

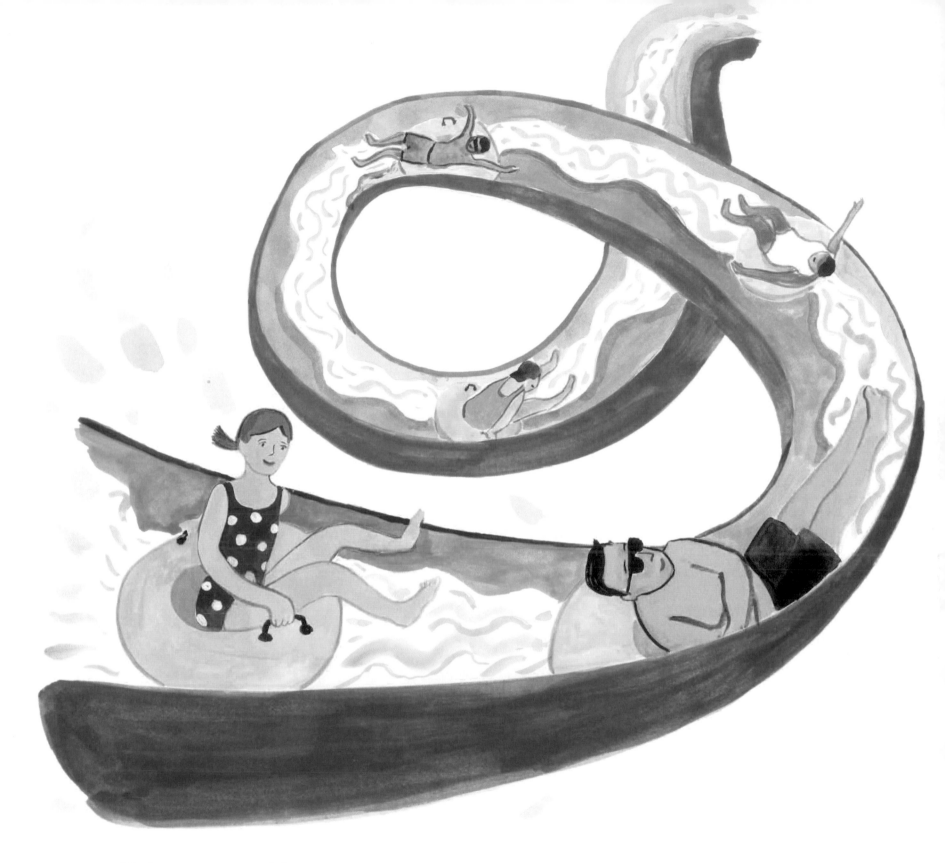

If the ramp could turn into an enormous water slide, she thought,
this museum would be very cool!

"Let's walk down the spiral slowly and look at the art," said Lizzie's dad.

A moment later, his cell phone buzzed.

"Lizzie, I have to answer this e-mail. It's very important. Will you please hold on to the stroller?"

"Sure, Dad!" She grabbed the handles and waited . . . and waited . . . and waited . . . for what seemed like a very long time.

"This is really boring," Lizzie said to her dad. "I'm going down the ramp with Ben."

Dad was so busy with his e-mail that he didn't hear a word she said.

Roy Lichtenstein, *Grrrrrrrrrrr!!*

As Lizzie pushed the stroller, she noticed something that looked like a comic in the distance. She went closer to see what it was.

Yikes! She was face-to-face with a giant growling dog! Lizzie thought the ferocious-looking beast was about to attack her.

She threw her hands up in the air to protect herself. Suddenly, the stroller began speeding down the spiral with Baby Ben.

Lizzie hollered, "HELP!" and took off like a rocket.

7

A tall museum guard heard her yell and quickly caught up to her.
"Why did you scream, young lady? And where are you going in such a hurry?"
he asked. "This museum has rules: No loud noise and no running!"

"I'm sorry, sir, but I need your help," cried Lizzie. "My baby brother is
in a runaway stroller, and it's speeding down the ramp!!"

"Of course, I'll help you!" said the museum guard.

So the museum guard and Lizzie chased the speeding stroller down the spiral.

All at once, there was a colossal crash as they bumped into an artist who was copying a painting of a table covered with bottles and fruit.

"Sorry! My baby brother is in a runaway stroller, and we're trying to catch up to him!" Lizzie explained.

"My still-life painting shall wait!" announced the artist as she threw her paintbrushes up in the air.

So the artist, the museum guard, and Lizzie chased the speeding stroller down the spiral.

Paul Cézanne, *Still Life: Flask, Glass, and Jug*

The stroller was headed directly at a teacher and her students who were admiring a painting of a lovely sleeping lady with a lavender head and a sculpture of a smooth, bald marble head that was shaped like an egg. The two heads looked the same, yet different.

As they got closer, Lizzie could hear the teacher saying, "Did you know that the artist Picasso was madly in love with that lady with yellow hair? And that white head was Brancusi's idea of the perfect woman?"

"She doesn't look perfect to me," Lizzie said to the guard. "She has a lot of missing parts!"

Pablo Picasso, *Woman with Yellow Hair*

Constantin Brancusi, *Muse*

Just at that moment, the stroller plowed through the teacher
and her students, knocking them over.

14

Alberto Giacometti, *Nose*

Next Baby Ben bolted by a bumpy brown head hanging in a cage. It looked like Pinocchio. He started laughing and tried to grab the head's long nose until he saw its scary, screaming mouth. Then Ben changed his mind and began to cry.

When the teacher and her students heard Ben crying, they jumped up off the floor.

"My baby brother is in that runaway stroller!" cried Lizzie.

"Maybe we can catch him," said the teacher.

So the teacher and her students, the artist, the museum guard, and Lizzie chased the speeding stroller down the spiral.

17

Marc Chagall, *Green Violinist*

The group sped past another painting. This one showed a man playing a violin on a roof!

"This picture has a green head, too!" Lizzie said as she ran by.

The teacher explained, "When Chagall dreamed about his childhood in Russia, he saw fiddlers with green heads."

Then they passed a picture with floating lines, circles, and triangles in beautiful colors. Lizzie slowed down to stare at the painting.

"It makes me hear music from the green man's violin," she said to everyone.

The teacher told Lizzie that Kandinsky made abstract paintings with just shapes and colors. He wanted people to hear music when they looked at his pictures.

Vasily Kandinsky, *Composition 8*

Joan Miró, *Painting*

All of a sudden, the stroller zoomed by some people with earphones who were listening to a tour. They were admiring a painting with bright colors and funny shapes and dots that looked likes scribbles.

"Did I just see another green face?" Lizzie asked as she flew by, and the teacher nodded yes.

Meanwhile, the people with earphones saw all the excitement,
and they wanted to help stop the stroller, too.
  So the people with earphones, the teacher and her students, the artist,
the museum guard, and Lizzie chased the speeding stroller down the spiral.

Suddenly, Lizzie felt someone staring at her. She turned her head and saw a picture of a strange-looking man. Lizzie thought she was going crazy.

"Another green face? Who's that?" she asked.

"It's the famous artist . . . Andy Warhol . . . that's his self-portrait . . . a picture he made of himself," the museum guard huffed, all out of breath.

"Andy should have brushed his hair for his portrait!" said Lizzie.

"He was known for his spiky hair and his Pop art," added the teacher.

Andy Warhol, *Self-Portrait*

Just when they were about to reach Ben, the stroller ran over
a tourist's foot and leaped up into the air!

23

Ben screamed, "Wheeeeeeeeeeeeeeee!" as the stroller started to fly across the huge hole in the center of the spiral!

Lizzie closed her eyes, held her breath, and wished, *Please keep my baby brother safe!* Then she opened her eyes.

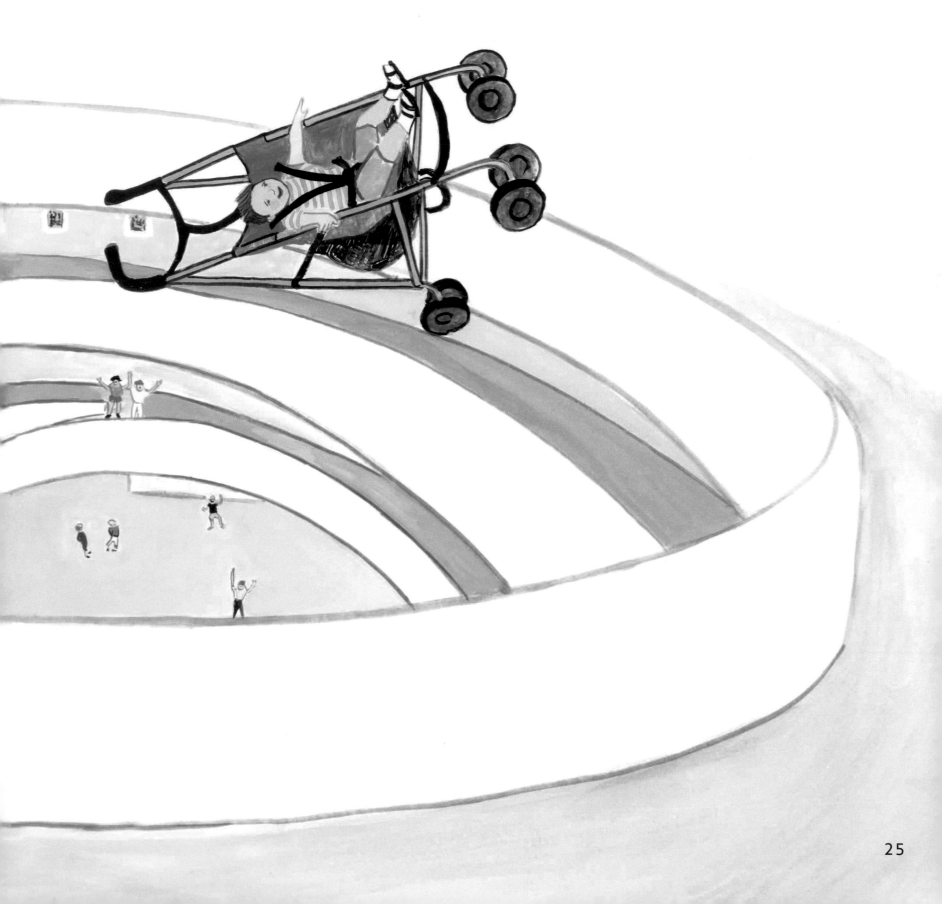

Phew! Ben had landed safely on the other side of the museum, but the stroller had banged into a big blue shelf on wheels, filled with hundreds of glass bottles. The shelf was now rolling behind Ben's stroller, and all the bottles were shaking and rattling.

What's a shelf doing in an art museum? Lizzie wondered. *Is that art, too?*

Louise Bourgeois, *Defiance*

Everyone rushed to the other side of the museum to catch up to the stroller and the rolling shelf.

As they got closer to the bottom of the ramp, Lizzie was afraid.

What if the stroller doesn't stop? she thought. *What if it goes out the door?*

27

Thankfully, the stroller crashed with a THUMP into a humongous heap
of black licorice candy.

Lizzie dove into the pile of candy to rescue Ben and gave him a huge kiss,
while the museum guard stopped the shelf before any bottles could fall off.

"This sculpture looks fragile, but it's strong. Just like Louise Bourgeois," he explained. "And she was eighty years old when she made it!"

The museum guard, the artist, the teacher and her students, the people with earphones, and the tourist collapsed with relief.

When they calmed down, the teacher told everyone about the pile of black licorice candy. "It's a contemporary sculpture by Felix Gonzalez-Torres," she said. "If you want to be a part of his artwork, you can take a piece of candy."

Lizzie took a piece of candy from the pile. It smelled funny. She preferred red licorice, so she put the black candy in her pocket to give to her father.

Just then, Lizzie's dad appeared. He looked very upset.

"Where were you, Lizzie? When I finished sending my e-mail, you and Ben were gone!"

Lizzie gave Ben and her father a giant hug.

"I'm so sorry, Dad. I got bored and went ahead, and then let go of the stroller by accident," she said.

Her dad listened carefully as she explained how frightened she was to see Baby Ben and the stroller Speeding down the spiral, and how many people tried to help.

"A work of contemporary art saved the day, and Ben is OK!" said Lizzie.

"You thought the museum would be boring. Instead, you had an *artful* adventure!" said Lizzie's father.

"Today was the coolest day ever! I hope we'll come back soon," said Lizzie.

"Sure," said her dad. "But next time . . . let's stroll down the spiral slowly!"

This imaginary story takes place at the famous Solomon R. Guggenheim Museum on Fifth Avenue in New York City. The great American architect Frank Lloyd Wright created this masterpiece of modern architecture, which took sixteen years to design and build. The museum opened in October 1959—six months after Wright's death. The building is white on the inside and outside. The giant spiral ramp is really cool and fun to walk down! Some people go to the museum just to enjoy the building.

All the fine art in *Speeding Down the Spiral* is in the Guggenheim's permanent collection.

I came up with the idea to write this book on a Sunday afternoon when I visited the Guggenheim Museum with my friend Beth and her four-year-old son, Zachary. As we got out of the elevator on the top floor, I wondered what would happen if we accidentally let go of Zachary's stroller. And that idea reminded me of an adventure story I had loved as a little girl—*Billy Brown: The Baby Sitter* by Tamara Kitt. I went home and immediately began to write so I could share my enjoyment of art and museums with other children and their loved ones. I asked Sophy Naess to illustrate my story because I thought her colorful, lively style would bring my words to life and be enjoyed by both children and grown-ups.

Hopefully, you will get to visit this extraordinary museum one day to experience the building and to see for yourself not only the paintings and sculptures featured in this book but many other great works of art. But please remember to walk slowly down the spiral, so you don't miss anything!

—Deborah Goodman Davis

CREDITS

page 7
Roy Lichtenstein
Grrrrrrrrrrr!!, 1965
Oil and magna on canvas
68 x 56⅛ inches (172.7 x 142.5 cm)
Solomon R. Guggenheim Museum, New York
Gift of the artist, 1997
97.4565
© Solomon R. Guggenheim Museum, New York

page 13
Pablo Picasso
Woman with Yellow Hair (Femme aux cheveux jaunes), Paris, December 1931
Oil on canvas
39⅜ x 31⅞ inches (100 x 81 cm)
Solomon R. Guggenheim Museum, New York
Thannhauser Collection, Gift, Justin K. Thannhauser, 1978
78.2514.59
© 2012 Estate of Pablo Picasso/Artists Rights Society (ARS), New York

page 11
Paul Cézanne
Still Life: Flask, Glass, and Jug (Fiasque, verre et poterie), ca. 1877
Oil on canvas
18 x 21¾ inches (45.7 x 55.3 cm)
Solomon R. Guggenheim Museum, New York
Thannhauser Collection, Gift, Justin K. Thannhauser, 1978
78.2514.3

page 13
Constantin Brancusi
Muse (La Muse), 1912
White marble
17¾ x 9 x 6¾ inches (45 x 23 x 17 cm)
Solomon R. Guggenheim Museum, New York
85.3317
© 2012 Artists Rights Society (ARS), New York/ADAGP, Paris
Photograph by David Heald © The Solomon R. Guggenheim Foundation, New York

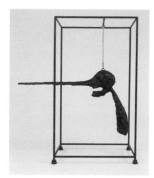

page 15
Alberto Giacometti
Nose (Le Nez), 1947, cast 1965
Bronze, wire, rope, and steel, edition 5/6
31⅞ x 38⅜ x 15 inches (81.0 x 97.5 x 39.4 cm) overall
Solomon R. Guggenheim Museum, New York
66.1807
© 2012 Alberto Giacometti Estate/Licensed by VAGA and ARS,
New York, NY
Photograph by David Heald © The Solomon R. Guggenheim Foundation,
New York

page 19
Vasily Kandinsky
Composition 8 (Komposition 8), July 1923
Oil on canvas
55⅛ x 79⅛ inches (140 x 201 cm)
Solomon R. Guggenheim Museum, New York
Solomon R. Guggenheim Founding Collection, By gift
37.262
© 2012 Artists Rights Society (ARS), New York/ADAGP, Paris

page 18
Marc Chagall
Green Violinist (Violiniste), 1923–1924
Oil on canvas
78 x 42¾ inches (198 x 108.6 cm)
Solomon R. Guggenheim Museum, New York
Solomon R. Guggenheim Founding Collection, By gift
37.446
© 2012 Artists Rights Society (ARS), New York/ADAGP, Paris

page 20
Joan Miró
Painting (Peinture), 1953
Oil on canvas
6 feet 4¾ inches x 12 feet 4¾ inches (194.9 x 377.8 cm)
Solomon R. Guggenheim Museum, New York
55.1420
© 2012 Successió Miró/Artists Rights Society (ARS),
New York/ADAGP, Paris

CREDITS *(continued)*

page 22
Andy Warhol
Self-Portrait, 1986
Silk-screened ink on synthetic polymer paint on canvas
106 x 106 inches (269.24 x 269.24 cm)
Solomon R. Guggenheim Museum, New York
Gift, Anne and Anthony d'Offay, 1992
92.4033
© 2012 The Andy Warhol Foundation for the Visual Arts, Inc./
Artists Rights Society (ARS), New York

The "humongous heap of black licorice candy" featured in the illustration on pages 28–29 is based on the sculpture shown above by Felix Gonzalez-Torres. The author thanks The Felix Gonzalez-Torres Foundation for granting Sophy Naess permission to re-create the sculpture in her illustration.
Felix Gonzalez-Torres
"Untitled" (Public Opinion), 1991
Black rod licorice candies individually wrapped in cellophane, endless supply, ideal weight 700 pounds (317.5 kg), dimensions variable
Solomon R. Guggenheim Museum, New York
Purchased with funds contributed by the Louise and Bessie Adler Foundation, Inc., and the National Endowment for the Arts
Museum Purchase Program, 1991
91.3969
© The Felix Gonzalez-Torres Foundation
Photograph by David Heald © The Solomon R. Guggenheim Foundation, New York

The "big blue shelf on wheels" featured in the illustrations on pages 26, 27, and 29 is based on the sculpture shown above by Louise Bourgeois. The author thanks the Louise Bourgeois Trust and VAGA for granting Sophy Naess permission to re-create the sculpture in her illustrations.
Louise Bourgeois
Defiance (Le Défi), 1991
Painted wood, glass, and electrical light
67½ x 58 x 26 inches (171.5 x 147.3 x 66 cm)
Solomon R. Guggenheim Museum, New York
91.3903
© Louise Bourgeois Trust/Licensed by VAGA, New York, NY
Photograph by David Heald © The Solomon R. Guggenheim Foundation, New York

GLOSSARY

An **abstract painting** is a picture that is created from the imagination of the artist. It does not have to look like anything you see in the real world.

Contemporary art is new art, not old art. Sometimes contemporary art can be confusing because it doesn't follow any rules. The artist can use anything to make art.

Pop art shows things from everyday life, like cans of soup, soda bottles, and even comics.

A **portrait** is a picture of a person. A **self-portrait** is a portrait you make of yourself.

A **still life** is a picture of things that don't move, like fruit, flowers, and bottles.

COLOPHON

The illustrations by Sophy Naess were painted with gouache on smooth bristol board.

The text type was set in Verlag, a typeface created for the Guggenheim Museum, and Brunella.

Manufactured by Color House Graphics, Inc., Grand Rapids, MI, USA

Edited by Joan L. Giurdanella

Designed by Erika Desimone

Communications by Jennifer Strikowsky

Production supervision by Beth Smith, A Life in Print, Inc.